I0713130

WRITING TO THE EDGE

prose poems and microfiction

edited by

Linda Godfrey
and Ali Jane Smith

SPINELESS WONDERS

www.shortaustralianstories.com.au

Spineless Wonders

PO Box 220

STRAWBERRY HILLS

New South Wales, Australia, 2012

www.shortaustralianstories.com.au

First published by Spineless Wonders 2014

Cover image and book design by Bettina Kaiser

www.bettinakaiser.com.

Copyediting and layout by Bronwyn Mehan.

Typeset in Franklin Gothic Book

Printed and bound by Lightning Source Australia

ISBN 978-1-925052-02-2

Catalogue-in-print

A823.4

Writing To The Edge prose poems and microfiction/

Godfrey, Linda & Smith, Ali Jane (eds)

WRITING TO THE EDGE

prose poems and microfiction

Why not go out on a limb? That's where the fruit is.

WILL ROGERS

Contents

INTRODUCTION

LAUREN AIMEE CURTIS

20   *dream baby*

JONATHAN HADWEN

22   *all that wasted heat*

PHILIP HAMMIAL

26   *Levitators*

NATASHA LUKA

27   *Punch*

ELIZABETH HODGSON

31   *Timeless crones*

KATHLEEN BLEAKLEY

32   *Purple basil/red feather*

ALYSON MILLER

35   *Stilled*

CASSANDRA ATHERTON

36   *White noise*

KATE ANDREWS-DAY

38   *Rue LaGrange, October*

JUDE BRIDGE

41   *Machinations*

PHILIP HAMMIAL

42   *Nudists*

JOSHUA LOBB

43   *Outside*

ALEXIA DERBAS

46   *Exchanges*

TIM HEFFERNAN

49   *jesus uses his camera phone*

MOYA COSTELLO

50   *The family regiment*

51   *On the ironing board*

SUSAN MCCREERY

52   *Fire Under The Skin*

MARJORIE LEWIS-JONES

56   *Pelts*

PHILIP HAMMIAL

58   *Family Reunion*

SUSAN MCCREERY

59   *Eight Seconds*

STEVI-LEE ALVER

63   *A pound of history*

RICHARD HOLT

66   *Her dark ground*

ROMANA DALGLEISH

67   *Circle space*

PHILIP HAMMIAL

69   *Tableau*

JENNI NIXON

70   *Disengaged*

ANDREW STUCKGOLD

72 *A drowning in the Tiber*

MARK O'FLYNN

74 *Percy Grainger's migraine*

MARK ROBERTS

76 *Cities that are not Dublin*

ALANA KELSALL

79 *the air we carry*

MARK SMITH

81 *10.42 to Sydenham*

BRENDA SAUNDERS

85 *Kafka's room*

JULIE CHEVALIER

86 *The man who walks after work*

PATRICK LENTON

89 *Phraseo- Rogue Editor*

KEVIN GILLAM

90 *Moth words*

RON PRETTY

92 *Trout*

NICK COULDWELL

94 *Westerly*

HILARY HEWITT

97 *Happy*

98 *Trolley Jam*

PHILIP HAMMIAL

100 *Slave*

BIOGRAPHIES

THE JOANNE BURNS AWARD

Introduction

A Tableau

How lovely: a widow with a feeding bowl. When we first looked it was empty. Now it's full.

Phil Hammial

Microfiction, flash fiction, short stories were the widows of the publishing world. Spineless Wonders has filled the bowl for readers looking for those small, delicious morsels.

A short work can be a mental splinter, working its way to the heart; a miniature world, masking the clockwork perfection of its mechanisms; an unforgettable square of rosewater-flavoured delight. The microfictions and prose poems in *Writing to the Edge* come in the form of stories, observations, evocations, under eight hundred words. There are strange and unsettling tales, playful games with words and ideas, narratives whittled into elegance.

This collection can be approached as a satisfying degustation, or a series of more-ish snacks. A riff on Percy Grainger inside a migraine, an ode to the ironing board, close encounters on public transport, a blue-eyed baby, paeans to dead sisters, private play with partners, respect to classic authors and a meditation on women who turn up to viewings of the dead.

So much of the work of bringing a book like this to publication happens online, but the kitchen table remains a vital creative space. The team of publisher, editors and readers Bron Mehan, Shady Cosgrove, Linda Godfrey, Ali Jane Smith, and Andrea Gawthorne met and drank tea and champagne and talked the book into existence around just such a table. As writers and as readers, we know how badly we need publishers who will take a punt on an unknown name, who will publish work that is new and strange and raw. *Writing to the Edge* is an opportunity for new writers to see their words in print, and for the old hands to experiment a little. Refreshingly different.

What Spineless Wonders doesn't want to do is underestimate our readers. We want to challenge your thinking, leave you with the taste of something new, yet recognisable so as to be palatable, to be thought about and chewed over, when readers understand themselves in the global. It's hard to pull off characters that are both personal and universal – but that was the core strength of this collection. We're taken beyond ourselves, and in that process, recognise ourselves.

To be published, whether on a page or a screen, means that a writer sees their work as the reader sees it, out in public, alongside other poems and other stories. Faults and flaws previously invisible will leap to the eye, but eclipsing all else is the scary-wonderful feeling that your work will be read, by people you've never met or heard of, now and perhaps even in years to come.

Without you, dear reader, this collection would be a coin dropped into an empty well.

Linda Godfrey & Ali Jane Smith

Editors, 2014

Lauren Aimee Curtis

DREAM BABY

We had a baby. In my dream last night we had a baby boy. It was lucid dreaming, so while everything circled around us, I knew that the baby was a dream baby and not a real baby. But for some reason this did not make him any less real. Physically, he couldn't have been our baby—he had blue eyes, he had blonde curly hair—he looked more like a small child, though he wore a bib and could not speak. He had the presence of one of those Renaissance paintings of the baby Jesus—adult head, baby's body, held by Mary—though I did not hold him. Instead he sat, wide-eyed in his baby chair, observing us.

In the dream, there were certain things we had to do. We had to fight certain people, when and if they appeared. It was important that we climb the Harbour Bridge. We had to complete these tasks, but we did not know what to do about the baby. We wondered if it was ok to leave the baby at home for a few hours. We knew you couldn't do that with real babies, but this was only a dream baby. So we left him alone. We left him alone more than once. And each time we returned he was exactly how we left him—sitting in his highchair, not speaking. Watching us with his big, blue, neutral eyes.

I worried about him in the dream but then I would catch myself worrying and tell myself to stop because there was no need, he was only a dream baby. And still, while we went off to fight strangers and climb bridges, I did not stop thinking about him. When we returned home for the last time they would not let us inside. The baby had died, they said. We'd left him alone, and babies cannot be left alone, they said, even dream babies.

We sat in your mother's living room knowing full well it was not your real mother. She had red hair and her accent was American, she poured us tea into little china cups. Her house looked like something floral had thrown up on it. When I told her about the baby I surprised myself by crying and the guilt ran out my eyes and my nose and my mouth. I told her because he was just a dream baby I thought he'd be ok. She asked me through her pursed lips why all my dreams were about unwanted pregnancies and older, lonely women.

Jonathan Hadwen

ALL THAT WASTED HEAT

The man who works at Coles was in a motorcycle accident. He walks crookedly now; his face is crooked. He is not smarter, but he is happier. He was angry before. He would ride his bike, a grimace behind his helmet, speeding up the straight and busy streets of this suburb.

*

The man in the apartment two doors down is not old; he is dying. I hear his coughing fits – they last for minutes – sometimes at the end he is sobbing, especially in the morning when he has been woken by the need for air.

Sometimes his young children visit. I never see their mother. They are loud inside the tiny apartment, running around its sharp turns. In the afternoon they leave, and it is quiet, except for his coughing again.

*

At the local cafe they keep their sugar in medicine bottles. It used to be in containers, but people would spoon out sugar with spoons they had sucked on, so they keep it in medicine bottles now. The necks of the bottles are too narrow for a spoon to fit. I shake a dose in my coffee. The coffee tastes like cream.

*

It is raining and I have forgotten my umbrella. I will wait at the cafe until it stops. I will order another coffee to keep the American waitress happy, or maybe browse in the bookshop next door. I will not buy anything; I have too many books already.

*

I am thinking of buying an old typewriter, but I am worried about the noise it will make, worried that it will annoy the girl downstairs, though she smokes on her balcony and the smoke drifts up through my windows, and this annoys me.

*

The rain is coming down in earnest now. Perhaps I will make a run for it. I wish I was in Paris.

*

The rain has stopped. I make my slow way home.

*

There was a man I used to see in the lunchroom, a mature-age doctoral student. In my mind I referred to him as 'Old John', because he was older than me, but not that old. He was very thin and used to eat spinach from his garden, which he would microwave with garlic and make the entire level of the building smell. He was a nice man.

I went overseas and when I came back Old John was gone. I assumed he had graduated, and I thought of him when I was eating my lunch in the empty lunchroom with its other smells I never noticed before. Six months later I saw an advertisement for a memorial prize in his name, his picture on a photocopied A4 poster.

I can understand that he is dead, but I can't understand those months when he was alive for me but already gone, pottering around his small house, reading, tending the plants of his garden.

*

I have a sore hip this week and I am understanding what it might be like to be old. It hurts every time I put weight on my left leg and I actually wish I had a walking stick to take some of the weight. I see a man with his walker, shaking his way into the front seat of a taxi as the driver waits to fold up the walker and put it in the boot. One day that will be me.

*

The man at the hostel next-door is telling the story of how he's been sick. He is drunk. He is drinking. 'I should be dead,' he says. 'They told me I should be dead.'

*

The man at the hostel finishes his story. The crow on the antenna begins his.

*

The sun comes out. Will the day begin in earnest now?

*

The basil plant on my balcony is going to seed. It has little flowers, and the stalk has become wooded, and the leaves are curling up. A nest of ants has moved in. They walk the wooded branches. I think they might be eating the leaves.

*

It is early afternoon but the sun is still coming in my front windows. It is winter and the sun's angle has changed. I could draw a blind for the glare, but I think of all that wasted heat.

*

I try to write a story set in England but the sun is out and the crows are out and everything says 'no, no, no'.

Philip Hammial

LEVITATORS

They seem to be multiplying. Hundreds, thousands eclipsing the sun, clogging up the air. It's becoming difficult to breathe. There ought to be a law against levitators.

Natasha Luka

PUNCH

The world swayed sideways. Cake stumbled towards the bin near the classroom door and coughed up the hamburger she'd had for breakfast. Sweat soaked out her skin and her mouth tasted like river slime.

'Jesus,' Skeg boy said, perched on his chair, as far away from her as possible.

Cake wiped her lips across her school blazer sleeve. 'Bloody Maccas.'

In her bedroom, Cake switched on the telly and tilted her head sideways. Her lazy eye made her look as if she'd been in a fight. A rush of warm air from the central heating vent flowed from the ceiling. Cake flopped onto a beanbag and dragged out a tray from beneath her bed. She'd been seasick all day. On the tray was a thumb size roll of foil and a clay pipe. She lit up and waited for the world to straighten out.

Her phone chimed. It was a text from Skeg boy. You coming, slut.

The falls gushed below in the darkness. On the cliff above, kids were sprawled out on the cold dirt in parkas and blankets. Cake sought out Skeg boy in his usual spot at the abandoned bluestone mill. A banana moon hung in the sky. Cake stretched out her fingers, trying to touch it.

'Brush your teeth?' Skeg boy asked, offering her the bong he'd made in metalwork.

Cake inhaled the bitter smoke, holding it deep inside her. Skeg boy undid his jeans.

Cake's ears popped. Cars headed into town, screeching wheelies against the gravel. She waited until all the headlights had disappeared and no one else was around. She glared at Skeg boy as he zipped up his fly.

'You got me pregnant.'

'Huh. How?'

'I need money.'

'I'm not giving you any. Could be anyone's.'

Cake reached behind Skeg boy, grabbing for his wallet. She clung to his jeans and dug her fingernails into his hip, trying to anchor him. He jumped and backed away.

'Crazy bitch.' He clenched his fist. 'Think you're so tough.'

'See how tough I am when I have it and hand it to your mum.'

'She won't believe you.'

'I'll get the test.'

'Like that proves anything.'

'Give me the money.'

'How about a punch in the guts.'

Cake stilled, the wind slowed and her seasickness made the rocky ground turn into a sinking mush.

Cake woke at 3 am and itemised her options. Her sinuses ached. The alien inside her wasn't going anywhere. Cake swiped on her phone and shone the light around her bedroom. She pulled on a woollen beanie and threw off the warm doona.

Barefoot, she shuffled along the chilled floorboards toward her parents' room. The room reeked of whisky sweat. She waited for them to breathe differently. When they didn't, she crept over to the jewellery box. She opened the pewter lid and reached in for her mother's eternity ring. Her hands were slippery and the lid clunked shut.

Her dad roared. 'What the—.'

Cake's heart lit up. She dropped the ring and bolted.

In the morning frost, Cake waited outside the chemist. School kids and mums with prams knocked past her. Her ears hadn't popped and everything sounded as if it were trapped under clouds of water. The footpath beneath her feet lurched like a floating pier. A woman in a floral shirt unlocked the chemist door.

At the counter Cake said, 'I need the morning-after pill.'

The woman eyed Cake. 'Do you have a parental consent letter?'

'No.'

'Go get one, then come back.'

Cake swung her school bag over her shoulder and bit back glassy tears. Her throat was so tight hardly any sound could squeeze through. 'Too bloody late anyway.'

Skeg boy wasn't at school. Cake waded through first period. The room swayed so severely she was unable to focus on the whiteboard. She peeled away her fingernail tips and scratched the crescent shaped spikes across her palm. The mid morning bell shrilled her awake. Cake stumbled out of the school gate and texted Skeg boy. Meet me at the mill.

On the crisp walk to the falls, Cake's ears popped. She broke off a eucalyptus leaf and inhaled its sharp-sweet scent. Skeg boy was at the mill, pacing and swinging his lanky arms about in the winter glare. When Cake reached him, she shoved him, hard, in the chest.

'Hey. I was only joking,' he said, palms upturned.

'Where's the money.'

'I can't get... that much.' Skeg boy's voice cracked.

A magpie cawed. Cake was out of options. She tied her hair into a ponytail and loosened her school kilt. She braced her feet on the dirt, and for the first time in weeks, the ground was solid, unwavering.

'Then punch me.'

Elizabeth Hodgson

TIMELESS CRONES

There's a group of women in your town, your city. It's not a large group. Sometimes it's a very small group. But it's a group all the same. Everyone, including you, knows of this group but no-one knows them. These women are old. Not just old like your granny. But old. Older than anyone else you've ever known about. And they're there at every funeral for an elderly person. No-one calls them. They know when to appear. They talk respectfully of the deceased. They eat all the little sandwiches. Drink all the tea. Don't offer them sherry. They will drink the whole bottle. One legend says that not one of these strange and ancient women will die. Another legend says they are already dead.

Kathleen Bleakley

PURPLE BASIL/RED FEATHER

For my sister Kerstie

18/12/72 – 29/3/11

Purple carrots

You are somewhere between us living and beyond. As we slept, you'd stopped breathing. My sister since our teens. My mum rings in the early hours. The day spinning on its axis. Ground wavering. My legs slowly moving. Swimming weightless inhaling & exhaling. Early autumn water reviving my skin. Sun, shaft of light breaking the surface crystals of you. We swam places where your pain flowed into the stream. You could dream of tumbling waves diving under. Skiing along them before your body got in the way. You became solid as the rocks you'd climbed. Still listening to the songs of dawn birds you'd soared with.

In the days following, I forget how to fork noodles into my mouth. Vegetables slide out of reach. But I catch your laughter, glimpse the purple carrots you grew. The plumcots you jammed, sweet, sour & lingering.

Postcard from Marrakesh

Dear Kerstie,

Orange trees line the streets of Marrakesh, pink city of mosaic places. Argan & olive trees scatter the arid stretches & lush valleys between here & the coast. Those cliffs that plunge into teal waters. If you were here, you'd swim; taste the nutty argan oil, feast on olives & baskets of flat, wholemeal bread. But you are in the light at dawn, the sun we bask in.

Purple Basil

Summer brings basil, purple your favourite colour. Days are fragrant, long and humid with grief. Tomatoes ripen slowly. So much rain. Our sweet corn grows taller than ever. You've missed the broad beans you loved to steam. They'll return next spring. If only you could. We would share this harvest with you.

Waves

Just as the waters are shifting towards tranquillity, a tidal wave. See it coming. Start to paddle. Breaking over my head. Pulling me under. Hard to see through depth of tears. Your earthly presence no longer anchored to us. You're riding waves of infinity.

Red Feather

One of the many roads of loss. Windows open to lingering summer. Red feather beside me. Approaching the first anniversary. Memorial gardens. Images of your cheeky smile in high school uniform. Cartoon socks at Christmas. Black & white waitress. Scarves & winter jackets at my birthday. Plum sisters – colours, flavours of fruit we shared. You grew & preserved. Your jam in the larder. Plenty sweet enough.

Red feather, light golden leaves lift in the breeze. And it's gone out the window.

Alyson Miller

STILLED

The colours of tea and clotted cream, a death sequence of digitized photographs—Victorian memento mori, families stood fist-tight around the bodies of their kin. Babies and small children, their tiny hearts and milkweed bones too friable for birth or winter, their skins mantle-light and translucent. Posed as though breathing, stone hands are locked around dolls or other fingers, clothes pressed and formal, and eyes painted onto lids that have not opened for days. In one, a twin holds the wrist of her sister like a promise, identical in gingham dresses; in another, a girl tugged into standing by metal rods and rigor mortis—her arm stretched as though to touch your face. I am reminded of another girl, her grief a strange and animal thing, showing me a photo on her father's phone of a sister that gave up seven months along the way. The neonate skull was half-eaten and collapsed, the body broken and curled in against exposed ribs, shell-like and blackened by clots. She carried the image like some precious thing, seeing only the snub nose of their likeness and wondering if the dead baby might have once remembered the feel of her voice as she pressed her mouth against the skin of her mother's belly and sang.

Cassandra Atherton

WHITE NOISE

You trace the vein of blue biro between my toes with your tongue. Swirling around my second toe. Wormish. You nip the tough skin on the ball of my foot, press your ear against my warm ankle. I think for a moment just how much I want you to take me ice skating. Just because I like the word 'rink'. Just so you can lace my white boots and hold my hand as I scream white puffs of air. Narnian Merry-go-round. But you will never take me ice skating. We only ever go to Smorgy's, The Ramada Inn or the Laundrette in Buckley Street – the one with the big tumble drier for doonas. I initial your earlobe with my saliva. Nuzzle your carotid pulse with the tip of my nose. You tug on the ends of my hair, your pointy hip bones burrowing into me. Urging me to reach for my blue biro. I scrawl the first sentence of *Rebecca* on your back. You guess it's Du Maurier by the time I get to the capital 'M' for Manderley. You take the biro from me and press the nib into the freckled pits behind my knees. I ask you to press harder. Pleading with you to write your words in my plasma. Clear, sticky, cherry-tinted words. 'For a long time I used to go to bed early'. I smile. My skin singing. I want you to continue, to cover me in Proust. But you get impatient and paw at my thighs. I always preferred yo-yos to madeleines anyway so I snatch the pen from you and draw a stave down your backbone. Curly treble clef beneath your jutting shoulder blades. I colour in the crotchets but semibreves have always been my favourite. You guess it is *La Wally* from the fourth bar. And somehow you know it is connected to my desire for ice skating. Snow. Avalanche. Stalactites and stalagmites. Once you told me an obsession with white could only lead to sickness or marriage. And you said that neither of those were appealing. Neither of them could bind you to me. I search for my mohair beanie under the bed. The one with the big pom-pom my nana knitted for me. As I search, you brand me with the overture from *Crazy for You* and I pretend I am a bass as you stroke my hips. For a moment you become the pointy stand that rests on the polished floorboards, supporting the bass. And then you are tired of games. So tired you refuse to list all the songs that have 'Lucy' in the title on the soles of my feet. I try to scrawl all the characters from the John Fowles oeuvre down your right arm but you are already packing the sheets into the laundry basket. You toss me my figure skating magazine while we dress. In silence. We leave the washing in the machine while we go to Smorgy's. Halfway through a bite of cheesy toast I blurt out, 'Nicholas Urfe'. You pick up your fork and scratch 'Sarah Woodruff' into my palm. Maybe tomorrow I will ask you to take me ice skating. Maybe tomorrow after you have written your blockbuster on my eyelids.

Kate Andrews-Day

RUE LAGRANGE, OCTOBER

'There's a sort of log-shaped goats' cheese; it'll fit easily in your sleeve, don't be ambitious on your first try,' he said.

We were standing on the footpath of Rue Lagrange in the brisk autumn breeze of Paris. Golden oak leaves lay sodden on the ground like a carpet; the wind carried the good smell of mulch and rose. Danny was holding his coat closed with one hand – the buttons were long gone – but with the other he reached out and squeezed my shoulder briefly before he turned and walked towards the supermarket.

I followed, remembering the first time I'd seen him properly was like this, walking behind him, my eyes tracing the curve of his back. I'd met him before, but I'd sort of glazed over him in the mass of people that drifted in and out of my life then. The first time we met I only saw his slightly wonky left eye that looked inward just enough to make it hard to tell if he was listening to you or someone behind you. It wasn't until a few weeks later, on the first Sunday of August, that he stood out suddenly and forever, and his eye and his big nose and his freckled, brown face made perfect sense.

It was the hottest week of summer and a bunch of us were walking along the cobblestones on the left bank of the Seine. The river was a rare blue to match the sky, the tall lampposts that lined the banks echoed in the water, and each bridge we passed formed a perfect circle with its own reflection. We didn't need to crane our necks to see the white, fluffy puffs of cloud floating above our heads; the whole world was spread beneath our feet. He was wearing brown jeans, one hand in his front pocket, moving with slow, even steps. His soft cotton shirt sleeves were rolled halfway up his brown forearms, the thin material sitting coolly across his straight, broad shoulders. One fraying shoe-lace jerked behind him with every step of brown leather on the cobblestones. I stared at his back, at the nape of his neck where his dark, thick hair tapered to a point just below the collar of his shirt. I wanted to slip my fingers around his neck, feel the soft, cool cotton where it met his smooth, hot skin. I wished he would turn around. I felt his quiet self and longed to be near it.

After that day we gravitated towards each other. We would sit on the steps of the Pantheon drinking cheap red wine from old jam jars until the small hours of the morning, listening to jazz on a portable radio he'd stolen in the Marais.

He didn't steal a lot, but I knew he stole some. He had been living on almost nothing for a long time, supplementing his diet of baguette and brie with stolen chutneys, cherries, roulades and jams. I asked him to show me how; it seemed like something we could share. Maybe it would set me apart. Now that I stood in front of a gleaming cabinet of cheeses, I thought about my life before I came to Paris, the taxes and bills and salary and diligence. I thought about how straight and narrow I had always been, and how ridiculous it was to commit a crime because a man's back was straight and his shoulders broad and his face kind. It was, really, a dangerous and stupid thing to do. Wasn't it enough to run away to Paris?

'Are you okay?' Danny said, suddenly at my elbow.

I looked at him, those freckles so wonderful in the bleached light, and his eyes a rich brown. He was frowning, worried.

'You can just walk away, if you want,' he said.

I could've cupped his face in my hands and kissed him, then. I could have pulled him close and waltzed with him around the store. I thought about the feast we would have in the park, surrounded by bare green rose vines that still held the scent of fat pink flowers, their petals littering the grass. The autumn sun would warm our shoulders, and the juices of chutney and whole tomatoes would drip down our chins. We would take this cheese and tear off chunks of it with our fingers and it would be salty and creamy against our tongues. We would feast like kings as the bells of Notre Dame reverberated through the soles of our feet.

We stared at each other for a long moment, and then I grinned.

'I'm gonna steal the shit out of this cheese,' I said.

Jude Bridge

MACHINATIONS

The multi-function device smugly spews perfectly collated, shiny, full-colour documents from its square grey mouth, accompanied by a soft mechanical humming designed not to disturb anyone, but it disturbs me, every gentle working noise of the machine is another nail driven into my brain – we've been instructed by management to use the device as an example, to follow its lead, to work all day without breaks, to respond to every command immediately and efficiently, to cheerfully accept unpaid overtime and to repair ourselves overnight – I send the device an order to print five copies of a memo, it sends a return email refusing to print anything further from me until my attitude has improved and suggests we meet face-to-machine in the carpark at midnight to resolve our differences – I agree electronically and armed only with a flash drive and my wits, stand shivering in the carpark watching the device roll slowly towards me, humming menacingly as it approaches, shredded paper dripping from its grey plastic jaws.

Philip Hammial

NUDISTS

in apple trees. They're becoming a real problem. Reach up to pluck an apple & you touch genitals. Embarrassing? Only for the apple eaters. The nudists don't seem to notice.

Joshua Lobb

OUTSIDE

He has to get out of the flat, to spend time outside. So he starts catching trains on the weekends.

He doesn't go anywhere. He's on a loop: round and round, into the city, way out west and then back into the city. He watches people get on and off. Bands of sunlight flash over the vinyl. Prams get their wheels caught on the lip of the doorway. Obstinate youths smelt onto the seats, their limbs splayed out at right angles. He sees the scowl of a tie-wearing twenty-year-old on his way to a weekend job; the sweat seeping through a fat man's shirt; the triumphant grin of the boy who makes it in the doors as they bleep shut. A man looks down a young woman's shirt; she's staring out of the window, oblivious. A dough-faced teenager reads the same paragraph in a book over and over again. She's using her train ticket as a bookmark. Her heavy-lidded eyes drop, her head nods down and then flicks up again. She blinks into the sun. She tries again. She runs her fingers along the page. She puts her feet on the seat. She's fast asleep.

He sees the train ticket flutter to the floor.

He watches the stations blur by, into the city, way out west and back into the city.

For a long time he stares at the back of a man's neck. The

neck is creased: white stripes cutting into tanned brown. There's a mole that looks like it will detach itself at any moment. There's a wisp of hair curling, above the barely-attached mole. It's moving in the breeze.

His dead eyes pour over nothing. He doesn't notice the bands of sunlight fading, the flicker of fluorescent lights coming on one by one.

It's dark. The colours come back: grey and navy blue, black smudges on the plastic walls. His joints pinch. The carriage is empty but the train is still clattering on. The train scrapes against the end of a tunnel as the train approaches a gloomily-lit station. He lurches up. He scans the floor: a grubby fruit drink bottle, half a newspaper, the fluttered train ticket. He picks it up. The doors bleep open and he steps out.

He's facing at a grotty wall-ad. He can't work out what the ad is selling. The air is thick and sticky and laden with the odour of asphalt. He doesn't know how long he's been standing here. Three figures on the platform: him, a grey-faced man folding back a newspaper and a woman sitting way down the other end. The next train is due to arrive in twenty-seven minutes.

He drawls along the platform. The woman on the bench is all angles: elbows protruding from her white shirt, rest unevenly on her pointy knees. The bench is near a rubbish bin. He has the fluttered train ticket in his hand. He flicks the ticket in the bin. The angular woman doesn't flinch. He loiters. She shifts her weight. He runs his finger along the creases of his neck. She snaps a look at him, gets up and moves away.

He looks to the right, up into the gape of the tunnel. Grey fading into brown into black. A set of lights, red and white. He blinks into the blackness. It has a kind of texture, this blackness, rough strokes of thicker black scratching into the flatter, cleaner black. It's a warm darkness, a solid mass, it hums with energy.He fills up with buzzing heat. The thicker black throbs. It's denser. Is the tunnel moving? Is the darkness closer? Is the air warmer?

There's the sound of cutting air. The deep echo of a man's voice. A grip on his arm. A murmur of admonishment. He's being led backwards onto the bench. It's the grey-faced man. The woman has disappeared. A relieved chuckle from the grey-faced man. The newspaper has fallen to the floor. The man goes to retrieve it. The man gives a glance back. Reassured, the man moves away.

The next train is due to arrive in two minutes.

He goes home. At home, he can lie on his dark blue doona and watch television. He can shake pasta in a plastic colander. He can close the sliding door to the tiny balcony and shut the light and the noise out. There's no warm buzzing heat drawing him towards the blackness.

It's much safer there, probably.

Alexia Derbas

EXCHANGES

Camilla is wondering whether she and Hanan will ever be able to exchange more than just smiles. They're home alone together and Hanan has made Camilla's favourite Lebanese meal of *wara-einab*, or stuffed vine leaves. Hanan piles her stepdaughter's plate with a generous serving. Camilla wants to know where Hanan learnt to cook this good. What else has she learnt? Camilla considers writing a list of things she wants to know about Hanan, but as she finishes her meal, she forgets to do this. They eat through their smiles.

Eating was all that was planned for the day. Their only other option is TV. They could diverge and do other things in solitude but, out of politeness, neither wants to make the move away from the other. Camilla's body is molded to the cushions of the lounge, her arm lying on the armrest. The television is off, but they face it anyway. Camilla doesn't want to choose what to watch. She would rather watch a show she doesn't understand than feel guilty for having Hanan do so.

Hanan sits stiff at the other end of the couch, waiting for something to happen. She is desperate for a prompt from Camilla, an icebreaker. She likes it when they smile at each other. Hanan hopes her stepdaughter will at least keep smiling. Camilla motions toward the TV, then the DVD player with an open palm, as if to say *put something on*. She is smiling. Hanan nods and in a shaky voice says, 'Okay' but doesn't move from her seat.

Camilla points at the TV, eyes open wide and eyebrows raised. *You choose.* As her smile straightens out, Hanan jumps up out of her seat. She understands now; Camilla wants her to turn everything on. Australians are rather lazy, thinks Hanan, but at least something is happening. She turns on the TV and DVD player with ease. The red power button on the remote is a universal symbol.

Hanan sits back down. Technology is humming. Smiles are confused. The golden Arabic DVD cases Camilla had been expecting are nowhere in sight. She realises she has just asked her stepmother to turn on the television. She panics. She is panicking about what Hanan thinks of her and whether it can be rectified. She is panicking about the future. Her head shakes violently. Her cheeks are suddenly hot. Nobody is smiling now, though Hanan is trying. They both think about time and Camilla's father returning from work and as their heads become clouded with thoughts in the differing intonations of their respective tongues they are at one in their anxiety. *This is how it is going to be.*

Hanan is now crying. She doesn't try to hide her tears as she gazes at the TV screen. She recognises the individual letters that make up 'No Signal' but they can't make her understand. She is using deep breaths to steady herself. The sound of loud breathing is better than the wailing she feels inside. But her chest begins to convulse.

Camilla rushes over to Hanan. Patting her back, she tells her, 'It's okay'. Hanan is bent over and the shaggy rug soaks up her tears. Camilla calls her dad and instructs him to be ready to translate. This is all his fault anyway. Hanan hears Camilla use her name and recognises the tone that she uses only with her father, bored but tender. Camilla gently prods Hanan with the phone.

Her shaky hand raises the mobile to her ear and Hanan greets her husband. As she listens, her body slowly rises into a perpendicular position. The sadness dissolves from her face leaving a reluctant, embarrassed smile. She puts season two, episode three of her favourite soap on. Hanan and Camilla are about to find out how Shadi is coping with his wife's affair.

Tim Heffernan

JESUS USES HIS CAMERA PHONE

jesus went to apec on thursday as he's had a long term interest in the asia pacific. given the traffic restrictions he decided not to drive so he dispensed with the motorcade and caught the south coast train to central station. he walked the way he always walks when he goes to sydney on a mission, following the traffic lights, the green man and the tripping *tu tu tu tu tu tu* for those too blind to see. he first came across the falun gung in hyde park and he watched them and their five poses and their patience, forbearance and tolerance made him think twice. he took himself to macquarie street and soon the road fenced him in to the intercontinental hotel and some black cars, a four wheel drive gmc flying a commonwealth flag and osama bin laden being arrested while the police demanded the id of digital witnesses. he captured the scene with his camera phone but the police blocked the best shot so he moved between the barriers down to circular quay for some seafood and typically after this type of walk, a couple of pints of guinness at the merchantile hotel.

Moya Costello

THE FAMILY REGIMENT

The family regiment had its wardrobe full: uniforms for School Days, Holy Communion, Confirmation, Basketball, Fancy Dress, School Concerts, Summer Holidays, Christmas Celebrations, Birthday Parties, Graduation. Home-made; handed down; passed on from other branches of the family; later, op shop and recycled or shop-bought. We slipped ourselves into these pre-given personas. The selection from the wardrobe told us who we were at times when we were unsure of this ourselves, or when we wanted to try out who we'd like to be. Sticking out from these 'dress-ups' – these cardboard cut-out clothes for paper dolls – are our faces, smiling, and our thin limbs. We are minimally secured and loosely wrapped by our uniforms which do and do not restrict us. Held and escaping, we are seduced and are not; we comply and do not. Then, our wardrobes featured the functional: shoes and suits for work. Though on some days still our beds are surfaced with regalia. For an hour or so, layer is thrown on layer, on a day we have missed our calling. We have not ironed the night before; we have not heard the weather nor listened to our intuition. And our clothes gather in mounds like funeral pyres, the death of various identities.

ON THE IRONING BOARD

We are on the ironing board in a set of our Fabulous Frocks. Aware of the performative, the Fabulous Frocks for display – gathered skirts flounced with fullness from cotton petticoats; collars standing out over shoulders; buckles on belts; bows and binding on collars; pockets on skirts; buttons on shoulders – we're house models like name brands, slightly bemused at our gathering. Our Fabulous Frocks are starched; our skin is cleaned and polished; our hair is watered down, caught with pins and tied with ribbons. We are stiff with formality. Our forced smiles show this. We are balancing on the ironing board. A date and time set. A photographer hired. We are hard pressed. We want to do our best. Our eldest sister's arms across our shoulders tells us this. And our Fabulous Frocks. Several flash bulbs later and a set of proof sheets show that heat from light and steam crushes too. Our bodies slip from perfect view—a strained lip droops; a tired eyeball shifts; a wisp of hair springs loose; a ribbon slides askew. Wrinkles and creases: we will wear these imperfections more often than we will grace. Ironing is no metaphor for living.

Susan McCreery

FIRE UNDER THE SKIN

Carl had visited a lot of specialists but none could give him an answer. It was as though fire-ants were tunnelling under his skin, he said. His skin was hot and crawling at the same time. He took long cold showers and would emerge mauve and dripping, treading wet footprints over the carpet. Towelling dry would only set fire to him, he told Clara.

Clara had begun to wonder whether the condition was all in his mind, but instead of suggesting this she bought a bag of ice and some watermelon. Both possessed cooling properties.

I'll slice it in a sec, she called from the music room. Just give me five. Then you might try an ice-bath.

She ran her fingers up and down the scales. Three days until the concert and she had not yet mastered the trills. Carl's condition was siphoning her energy. Her fingers appeared to be stiffening with stress.

Meanwhile, next door, the bearded man had taken to tap-tap-tapping without recognisable rhythm in the evenings. Indescribable the effect this was having on the already charged air in the apartment.

On the day of the concert Clara ran a hot bath, and while she was waiting she took in her dress at the waist. She planned to luxuriate in the water, and flex and unflex her fingers while playing the entire concerto in her head. Carl was out roaming the streets, collecting pieces of aloe vera for his skin.

She snipped the black thread and stowed away her sewing basket.

What with the intermittent tapping, Carl's skin and her calendar filling with bookings, Clara felt boxed in like an insect. The truth was she loved Carl and perhaps therein lay the problem. Perhaps this love was an inhibitor.

While she was in the bath her manager called to say they'd almost filled the seats. For a newcomer this was sooo promising, he squeaked onto the answering machine. He also said that the trio from South America booked to appear before Clara had been spotted drinking tequila in the neighbouring bar and one of them showed signs of being hammered.

Clara listened to the message then lowered her head into the water. What was it she'd been thinking about earlier? About love being an inhibitor. If she utilised the same amount of energy on her practice and on her composing as she did on loving Carl, her career could quite possibly fly.

A muffled knock at the door. She ignored it at first, but it grew insistent and besides it was possibly a delivery – natural or unnatural remedies ordered online. Carl wouldn't appreciate having to collect the package from the depot.

Bathrobe on and hair swathed in a towel she opened the door to see the bearded man from next door.

My name is Jovan. I am neighbour.

I know. Your car space. I've seen you.

Your music. Jovan opened his big hands to the ceiling and moved them side to side. He appeared to be struggling for words. It is very special. To me.

Oh. I'm sorry. My music room should be soundproof – *no noise.*

I hear very small. Small sounds. But I know it.

Where are you from?

Serbia.

Clara nodded. Well. Thank you. You must come to one of my concerts.

That would be special.

Well, if you'll excuse me.

Wait one minute.

Jovan reached behind him and placed before her a three-legged wooden stool, topped with a plush red velvet seat rimmed with heavy brass studs.

For the music, he said, and with a nudge of his hand he gave the seat a twirl.

Just then Carl appeared in the corridor with a basket of cuttings.

Carl, this is our neighbour, Jovan. Look at this piano stool he made for me.

Carl grunted and scratched himself. So you're the one making the racket.

Racket?

Noise. Bim, bim.

Yes. Very sorry. Jovan shifted his feet. Well, goodbye. Nice in meeting. Music beautiful, he added.

You were particularly unpleasant to Jovan.

Carl, stripped down to his shorts, had split open the aloe leaves on the bench, revealing their jelly innards.

Do my back?

You can't be serious, said Clara. Look at me.

Carl surveyed her black dress. Put on an apron. I'm on fire here.

Clara slapped a leaf to his back and smeared it across his skin. You have to get dressed. We have to go.

I can't put a shirt on over this stuff.

Clara tossed the mangled leaf into the sink and wiped her hands. She took her purse from the piano stool by the door. She slowly rotated the stool, humming the concerto's opening bars. Then she draped her shawl, dusk-red, round her shoulders.

Hey! said Carl. Come back. I'm burning here. I'm burning alive.

Marjorie Lewis-Jones

PELTS

And then we came to a cabin. It had been raining and we'd lost the path. We knocked and found there was no one in. The door was unlocked. We entered. Our eyes adjusted to the gloom. There, on the walls, were the pelts of scores of animals. They were hung as if to keep the cabin warm; hanging there without threat or accusation, benign and soft to the touch. We touched them first with our hands and then with our cheeks. I laid the side of my head against one pelt and slid my hand across to stroke the next one. It seemed easy to stay like that—with my head resting and my hands stroking the fur—for a very long time. I could not remember when I had last felt that comforted. The room, the pelts, the sound of the rain on the roof and the lack of speech; all these things calmed me. I could have easily drifted into sleep. Pelts with tails hanging—there for the stroking. It did not enter my mind that they had once been living animals whose little hearts beat in panic as they were hunted down. It did not strike me then that someone had loaded a gun and whistled up his dogs and gone into the forest to kill these creatures and line his walls with their fur. I do not know why this aspect of the experi-ence only came to me much later—an old man looking back over my life and recalling the extraordinary things I had done and seen. Perhaps it is stranger still that my companion and I never spoke of what happened in the cabin that day. That I did not ever dilute this memory through speech meant it became, over time, a kind of shrine in my mind, a talismanic vision—a work of art. At significant points in my life's journey I returned to the image, cajoling it to work its magic; especially on those dark days—the doom days—when the lawyers and other predators gathered on the horizon, sharpening their knives. The pelts have been there for me, like good friends, a number of times since that rainy day in the cabin and I recall each *visitation* with clarity and fondness. I often dwell on the possibility that they could outlast me. I get extremely distressed if I contemplate the destruction of the pelts, either through decay, infestation or being ripped from the walls and buried or burned. I can offer no explanation as to why I so fervently want to preserve the corporeal aspects of an encounter that has lived so discretely in the recesses of my mind these past decades—an encounter in a place I never revisited in person. I used to puzzle over this, even fret a little. Now I accept it as a mystery. In their dying days, many men wish only to be held close by their wives or partners or surrounded by their loving children. My wish is to feel those silken pelts, to see their bright and beautiful hues and to inhale their rich, animal smell as I lie in my death chamber: To receive their consolations one last time.

Philip Hammial

FAMILY REUNION

Aunt Jane is in father's bed. Uncle Jack is in mother's bed. I'm in
bed with seven cousins, male, female & trans. Who will do what
to who is anyone's guess.

Susan McCreery

EIGHT SECONDS

All you need is eight seconds a day, said Gareth. Twice. Or three times.

What a deal! she said. At Tony Di Milia flooring we have: Parquetry, Hardwood, Cypress Pine, Pelvic.

Gareth joined in the spirit of things.

I'd like three centimetres of Pelvic Flooring, please.

As new, she said. Hard-wearing. Long-lasting.

Tongue and groove. Tight joins.

At Tony Di Milia we don't beat around the bush.

Slight imperfections are part of the charm.

Five babies, she said, suddenly sullen. What do you expect?

Gareth reached under the table and put his hand on her knee. I am so lucky.

His fish arrived a few seconds later.

Funny, she said. You never ask for fish at home. Do you think we know all there is to know about each other? Without our children, who are we? She paused. Let's talk, then, about the things we'd like to fix in each other. My turn. The way you scratch me. I hate scratching. Well, not scratching as such, but pulling your fingernails along my skin. It's intensely irritating.

The way you gulp. Oh my God. I hate it when you gulp fluids.

You have skinny eyes. Remember that movie? The kid said, *He has skinny eyes.* They're not that skinny, by the way. But sometimes you have this blank look. Like you're not all there. Adrift. And you don't smile enough.

Your smile is not always genuine when you greet someone you know in the street. Why pretend you're pleased to see them?

Why be so rude as to stand there with your blank look?

Gareth separated a bone from fish flesh and placed it carefully on the side of his plate.

Your wide hips, from the back, look like a giant soup tureen.

A wet pall of silence. She took a loud gulp of champagne.

Here's to us.

Cheers, he said, not disguising a grimace. After a moment he said: There's a man at the bus stop in the morning who's very old. Maybe a hundred.

That's old.

Can you imagine being that old?

You mean me? Or us.

No one in particular. You.

So I'm no one in particular?

You take offence too easily.

That comment was never on any of my report cards. Straight As. Even for Attitude.

Up until then she'd only toyed with her eye fillet, but now she took the steak knife and swiftly hacked off a hunk and began to chew viciously.

The six translucent bones Gareth had eased from the fish lay in a neat row. He pushed the spinach puree to one side with his knife and skewered a baby potato.

I'm doing it here, now, she said, without looking at him.

Everything to your satisfaction? The waiter alongside in her black apron. Flat-bellied, slim-hipped.

What should she say? No. It's hideous. We're having a hideous time. My husband would like my vagina to be as tight as yours. I want him to smile more. I'm sitting here doing an eight-second pelvic floor exercise as I nod that everything's perfect, thank you.

After the waiter left, Gareth reached into his smart jacket pocket and pulled out a small blue box bound with a silver ribbon. With an expression that was loving, pinched and wary he pushed the box across the table, saying, Happy Anniversary.

Have you noticed how Robbie has been rolling his eyes? Like this? she said.

Gareth shook his head and glanced at the box.

Maybe take him to the optometrist.

That's not what he needs. I think he's anxious.

Are you going to open it?

In a minute. Don't you think he might be anxious?

About what?

He's picking up on the atmosphere.

What atmosphere?

Would you care for dessert?

Could you give us a minute? said Gareth to the black apron. He then leant forward and whispered, almost hissed: Why don't you open it?

She looked away and saw how, outside, through the vast window, the sky was a suffused rose on blue and the moon, which had risen, was resting on the blue part, which made it foam-white in contrast. She wondered whether it was full or whether there was the slightest shaving off its edge, and even while she was wondering this she was also aware of how dog-tired she felt.

She looked down at the box in front of her and heard Gareth exhort her once more to open it. She did not want to open it. The question was: How could she come up with a reason not to? She would give herself eight seconds.

Stevi-Lee Alver

A POUND OF HISTORY

After Gertrude Stein

GIVING

The wind is breath that is laughter not in wind but in storm, in storms of laughter. A kind of grey in a cloud, a form of mist framed by the sky, a hue of lonely-black smudged above her. She is nothing still. Nothing quite still floats. And floats with grace. Oceans fold at her sides like sheets gathering. Seasoned sheets fold like autumn leaves falling. All this and salty lips not unnoticed.

Seasons unfold as they stand and watch and want and want to take what is not theirs. A softly scented season is not theirs. Not theirs beneath an origami moon. Not theirs a drifting barren figure. What is there is what there is in what there is to come. That is theirs.

MATTER

Sunny *terra nullius* dissolves the night sky. Only in darkness do shining stars shine. Closed eyes see visible invisibility. They matter. In her palm they squat like brail.

From her palm green-frog leaps, stick sticky pad hand. Through space green-frog leaps, stick sticky pad feet.

The space in that is that she is the space they see. There is that which came before. There is that which cannot be seen. A history in land is that in that that is her, hers, her and hers. She is invisibly visible. In that she sleeps. She sleeps. Asleep, sleeping pregnant with her future's history.

STORM

Ice-breath lingers but does not blow. If breath is not windy then a dangerous laugh is not heard. If wind does not blow then danger is silenced in a wind that deflates. Winded by a single gift already given, her breath catches slowly. In dawning doldrums her deflated frame sits. Her wind is not defeated, not defeating in not conforming. Her wind is not tangled, not untangled in nothing like entanglement.

A breathless wind slips through fallen sheets and gathering leaves. A flame is fuelled in loneliness. A flame is petrified in a lonely breath. A breathless orchestra's wind burns in arpeggios. In birthing breath of windy passions laughter is born. The wind is born in that space that is not wind but in space, space of wind. The wind is born in storms of laughter.

PENALITY

Prisoned in floating prisons are prisoners at sea. Unhulled in a dark space, only touch to see. Light blinds the sightless in dark places. Forsaken spaces. Captive convicts. Convicts captive but not captivated by deserted desert-blazes. Unbelonging blaze. Petrified flames. Boats float prisoners don't. Blinded prisoners sink in seas of uncertainty. The uncertainty in that of searching is that uncertainty in that that is hope. The search was over and she was lost. Lost is not only to lose but to locate. And to occupy like gravity unexplained. And colonise like blood dripping. Dripping. Dripping and filling newfound space.

POUNDING

Ten-pound handed, not only handed but taken and not only taken but navigated away. Ten-pound empty pockets, ten-pound per piece, children free. Ten-pound per piece, twelve pence per shilling, twenty shilling per pound, pounds of profit, pounding profit, children free. A piece was not a pound, not a bit of it. A piece was pounded. A piece was not exchanged, not a bit of it. A piece was taken. A piece was not left over, not a bit of it, not at all.

Richard Holt

HER DARK GROUND

Adelie kept a locked book of recipes for black. Thirty or so, each with its mood and purpose.

Every canvas she painted began as one of these shadowy combinations. Choosing the right one, mixing it, spreading it over white gesso, was all that kept her painting. And painting was all that kept her. Only when her chosen ground was as close to perfect as she could make it would she obliterate it beneath the effusive colour around which her reputation had been built.

Romana Dalgleish

CIRCLE SPACE

You were hours away on an airplane and my mouth was bleeding, I think I'd bit my cheek. I was on the train, running late for work. The train was stopped between Richmond and Flinders Street, I hate it when it does that. I was interrupting your work with messages about bloody mouth kisses. I can't remember what you wrote back but I had to put my phone away. The smirk cartwheeling across my face was a beacon making sure every stranger sitting next to me knew my tummy was a somersault.

The tram driver is waving his arms around. There is a girl walking in front of the tram, soft gait, slow pace. Small with big head-phones, she walks with her head down. The tram driver has been ringing the bell but she doesn't respond, keeps moving, committed to each step. There is a tram going in the other direction also waiting for the girl to pass; that tram driver is laughing. Our tram driver is still waving his arms in the air. He is pretending to twirl his hair, impersonating the girl who doesn't look. Moving away slowly, she doesn't see.

In a space so full of bodies we are almost anonymous. You are a girl becoming a boy; I am a girl wondering how it feels to want a boy that used to be the girl you love. The blond woman sitting opposite us looks out the window as our conversation falters. We are taking sides in other people's stories. A girl we knew from school had a girlfriend who became her boyfriend and then they broke up. You say it was harsh the way she left him. I say one day out of nowhere the woman you love says I'm going to be a man, don't touch me like that, don't call me that name. Would you stay with someone who didn't let your life together be a part of their decision-making, who didn't let you know until it was already happening? You say it wasn't about her, that it is bigger than that. And maybe it is. You say going on T has nothing to do with anyone else. You're speaking loudly, including everyone around us in your thinking. If you wanted testosterone it would have nothing to do with me.

The tramfull of people we don't know, going who knows where, breath in time with me. You don't want to be a boy but that's not what we're talking about. You're making sure I know that your choices are all yours because all of a sudden you're not sure if they are. Looking anywhere but you, I arrange the words that would ask you to think of me when you make decisions. Nervous, they wait behind my teeth. Instead I say you're aggressive enough without extra boyhormones and quietly hope that you'll come over after work.

Philip Hammial

TABLEAU

How lovely: a widow with a feeding bowl. When we first looked it was empty. Now it's full.

Jenni Nixon

DISENGAGED

as part of the new welfare income management scheme we find you in breach of your centrelinkup agreement. i am compelled to inform you that our electronic data compromised due to a recent proposal implementation relating excessive oversight by bureaucratic interference in family payments find you disengaged and must be helped to get the benefits of income management. this cannot be completely voluntary. we glean purchases traced via barcodes reveal you exceeded recommended fatty food guidelines as established in your online health dossier by health care professionals. as a consequence the department of homelandcare require us to limit access to all take-away pizza fish and chips and hamburger purchases. we are committed to delivering fair and equitable procedures so as a sweetener the longer you stay quarantined we will provide an incentive—every six months we will review our decision to suspend all payments and you may have your benefits reinstated if you consider refraining from alcohol cigarettes the pokies and

try feeding your children broccoli. we also expect
that if you do not comply you may place in jeopardy
all future supplementary allowances until further
notice (see our enclosed fact sheet). you may want
to call us between business hours. we wish to advise
our tribunal will hear complaints should you seek
independent advice about your rights and obligations
under your centrelinkup contract.

yours sincerely

client service officer

---

on behalf of the minister

Andrew Stuckgold

A DROWNING IN THE TIBER

There is a kind of river of things passing into being, and Time is a violent torrent. For no sooner is each thing seen, then it has been carried away, and another is being carried by, and that too, will be carried away.

Marcus Aurelius, Meditations, Book IV, 23.

We descend marbled stairs that smell sharply of human excrement; and under the Ponte Sisto there is a derelicts' camp; not soldiers but rag men, ignobles, burning river rubbish to heat food.

In the slow light of the still distance a rowing scull slides downstream across the green clouded mirror of the river: and here the occasional gull stoops or a lone fishing bird vanishes momentarily beneath the waters. At intervals along the packed earth or cobbled stone plane of the high walled shore there are open air restaurants, small cafes and kiosks. Most it seems are closed, jumbled; empty.

At first we think he might be swimming; such a strange thing to be doing at this time of year and in this seemingly broken river.

As we look closer we begin to understand: this is a dead body floating in the slowed waters; a body with gravel damaged hands and feet. It is naked except for a pair of sodden white underpants like a clout. A watery cloud of tangled hair obscures the head and face, and a length of rubber tubing is tied off around one discoloured, lolling stick of an arm.

High above us now, near the farther bridge, the smokers among the trinket selling illegals have noticed; they lean curiously over the wall, intent on a closer view. An old woman on the Trastevere side, a gelato seller, is beginning to yell over the tumbling sound of the weekday traffic:

'Gesù, una persona annegata, una persona annegata nel fiume, un corpo!'

We stand in the river's wide stone gully. We are frozen; appalled at this extraordinary vision. The body floats to a swollen halt for a moment in front of us; then it turns lazily sideways and rolls face down: and now the river might almost be quietly mumbling in half forgotten Latin as it gently moves it on.

This pale corpse; this remainder of some unknown; a momentary speck of human circumstance: it is drifting on the slow current downstream toward Ostia, toward the anonymity of the open sea.

Apartment on Via Angelo Tittoni, Trasteveri October 2012

Mark O'Flynn

PERCY GRAINGER'S MIGRAINE

Those loud throated, bronchial horns sketching charcoal on the footpath. Reduced to keening, blunt and battered, raw and sweet, he gargles and pants, poor chap, like a clown in his dandruff. The morning ratchets whir, his toasty whiskers scrape against the silk of your thigh. Outside the sandals slap the sunlit steps of the basilica. The twiddling finger bones of saints beneath the holy slick on the lake pluck the fish gnawed harp strings of his nerves. His slippers shuffle in the kitchen's hollow shoe spoons and the rattling jigsaw loosens a percussion of cutlery on the sharpening stone of the goat-greased altar.

The leaning candle flames flicker to the dancing clogs of the peasants. What on earth is that stench coming from the scullery? Feet pounce, claw, cling, stamp, pirouette, bleed. How, in the steel booted factory, does this translate? His asthmatic flutes wheeze their thin finches weeping, trickling the refrain. White noise amongst the ironwork, a widow's veil at toppling. Dark on a moonless night, the bass owls purr their mutiny.

Corsets. Wishbones. Scapulars. Fever savours its pathology. Sparks fly from the anvil through the fog-slurried windows. His sabots pace the length of the keyboard, while in the cellar the blind maids work to the deaf cook's drumming. *Tweak* and *plunk* and *boing*. Soprano horses whinny on the treeless heath. Hessian bags potato full of febrile chords melting at one and apart through the wisps of smoke. Peasant girls stir the black cauldron full of horsemeat and vegetables, and all thought stops for the soup's song.

Feral tubas huff across the acrylic lawn. Bilious trombones burp and gurgle over stewpots. What music is this? A single note's piercing light? A tintinnabulation of water. A trumpet bleats in the high matchsticks of the attic. The velvet air devoted to spittle and mist tramples across the skulls of the choir. The monks murmur behind their oak hands, the beads clatter like hailstones.

The death trumpets bark their *moribundus mori* while the sour old fellows clutch their dishcloth skirts like hags bogged in mud, bereft of harmony. *Tweak* and *plunk* and *boing*, the B-flat of the blood. Frost cracks like sandpaper or sandstone. The leadlight shakes its apparitions; smoky leaves blacken and curl, pyre flung clefs. Votive music fills the tabernacle with fly spots. Still the monks kiss their fists on the prayer worn flagstones. Silence as the pallbearers prepare to hoist the catafalque.

His fingers strum the cardboard. His feet are stricken with quills. His marrow ice to intention. Moan monks—grizzle, sneeze, bless. Even when the bolted timbers decay beyond the city's fixed hinges, every pounding feather alight, the last hiss of sun.

Mark Roberts

CITIES THAT ARE
NOT DUBLIN

i have a plan for reading ulysses—actually more than reading it, finishing it. today i am going to neilsen park with a picnic lunch. i will start reading next to the harbour, easing my way into the sections i have already read. then tomorrow night i am travelling to melbourne by train and plan to sit up all night and read.

i make good progress, sitting against an old morton bay fig, reading familiar pages, looking up occasionally at a city which is not dublin.

*

the train is called the spirit of progress. it has dark brown leather seats, and the blue vicrail carriages look out of place at central station. there is a little reading light above each seat that can stay on all night.

i read for hours and sleep briefly in the early morning. i am thick into joyce when i sit up at the bench in the restaurant car and eat breakfast as the train emerges into the morning.

*

central dublin connolly   strathfield   tara street

moss vale   dublin pearse   goulburn   lansdowne road

yass junction   sandymount   junee   sydney parade

wagga wagga   blackrock   the rock

dun laoghaire mallin   albury   sandycove & glasthule

wangaratta   bray daly   benella

 kilcoole   spencer street   gorey

*

i am staying in marie and andy's flat in fitzroy street, just above leo's spaghetti bar. they have gone away for the weekend & i have the place to myself.

the flat has a curved balcony & large windows over looking the street. andy's drum kit is in the corner and three of marie's paintings are hanging on the wall. the largest is of a crumpled tube of toothpaste.

*

on my last night in melbourne i go to a party. it is in high street armadale & marie gives me a lift in her old mazda. the party is at the back of a laundromat which is still open when we arrive.

a strobe is is cutting the party to fragments and slinging them three a second through cracks in the door. hip melbourne boys are wearing pointed black shoes & all the girls seem to be dressed in orange and green. i start talking to the only woman dressed in jeans. she works at the local community radio station. when she learns that i am catching the train back to sydney in the morning she gives me a crunched up ball of foil. harsh crumbs for the trip she tells me.

as i leave the party walking past the now closed laundromat i see the street lights reflected in pools of water along commercial road. a couple is having an argument at a tramstop. he is yelling that he loves her. she is yelling at him to fuck off. they are holding hands.

*

sunset leaving goulburn. sydney just over an hour away. i swallow the last crumbs of the hash,and wash it down with a swig of vodka. i want to be ready for the lights of sydney's outer suburbs.

Alana Kelsall

THE AIR WE CARRY

for my sister spinner and weaver 1948 – 2012

at the top of the pines seeing more like a bird with the air we
carry cockatoos flying low over the dry grass the river a rag of
shadows between the gums hands in the sink Mum says we
can be anything we want even Grace Kelly my sister snorts I'm
not waiting for any prince I'm going to live in a tent we saddle
up every day fighting for our escape with jerky fingers the ponies
whinny to each other buck us off sometimes I think they laugh
she sniffs as if we have everything just a bit of air knocked out
of us Dad takes a deep breath before his talk about the right
way to do things or walks off I don't know which is worse follow
my sister everywhere for the road out *he loves me he loves me
not* pulling off the petals of cakeweed twining them into chains
this strangeness inside us what holds and twists however bright
the day is waiting for the slide down to summer the long trek
to a house near the sea leaving Dad behind on bushfire alert
the wind whipping our hair into each other's mouths four in the
back two in front the boot squashed tight on the kitchen sink

of buckets and pots and guitars old stones rattling inside me about whether I matter how to pin the day down can't get it right daybreak the drumming on the wooden floors the jump with the air we carry down to the beach line up the towels rush headlong into the spray one striped windbreak like a flag to hold the six of us bobbing in the waves Mum's sun glasses call us back there are rocks round the headland caves we can get lost in carrying our own air my sister sniffs wanders off shell bucket in hand I come up the steps from the Tube sun light moving like a crease along the river concrete edges packed with people sipping at drinks in the forecourt of a hall a tree sculpture with the poems of asylum seekers fluttering like prayers she is so hard to call back now the heart seeker I don't know why love gets choked up I've been waiting for a destination I never had this is where our ancestors set out against banks of clouds towing their watery fields south towards a turn in the light somewhere promised unfenced she moved the furthest away of all of us a light touch on the reins knowing what she wanted what she'd move away for inside the hall an MC welcomes a Yorkshire singer up on stage I push past tables towards the back pale windows the light bitten out the singer unhooks her first note catches the band's slow metallic beat her voice tumbling into mouths bringing whole rows to their feet bags roped over shoulders faces tilting back I can almost get it the lift as I jump up winched with this basket of air thinking I can do this I can be out there with the give of this breath

Mark Smith

10.42 TO SYDENHAM

The air shifted the moment the three boys boarded the train. A man in a suit lifted his newspaper to cover his face; a young man slid low in his seat and disappeared from view.

Swinging on the overhead bars and climbing across the seats, the boys moved through the carriage.

Gabriel sat upright in his seat. He looked at the window and studied the boys in reflection. They were dressed uniformly, their jeans slung low and the tops of their underwear showing, tee shirts and black canvas shoes. He thought they had dressed with care.

The boys stopped half way down the carriage and encircled a girl sitting on her own. She adjusted her dress, pulling it down towards her knees. She didn't lift her eyes as the tallest boy hung from the overhead bars, swinging his feet in front of her face. Annoyed, he dropped into the seat opposite her. The other two squeezed in beside her, leaning in until they were almost touching her.

The tall boy pulled a packet of cigarettes from his jacket pocket and made a scene of cupping his hands against the non-existent wind to light it. He inhaled deeply and, leaning forward, blew smoke into the girl's face. When she still refused to meet his eyes he moved closer and put his hand on her shoulder. She shrugged it off and tried to stand up.

'Where the fuck are you goin'?' he asked, pushing her back down.

She looked to the other passengers. Gabriel met her gaze and nodded.

'Mine's the next stop.' Her voice was strong. Defiant, Gabriel thought.

'We're goin' through to Albion. Maybe you should come with us,' the tall boy countered.

'Ya gonna do 'er Simmo?' One of the other boys had found his voice.

'Dunno yet. Might catch somethin'.'

Gabriel remained motionless. He counted the seats between him and the group. Six. He turned his head to watch again in reflection.

By the time he was their age he had killed more people than he could remember. Women, children, old men, even a few soldiers. He was thirteen when he started. The white woman at the tribunal had cautioned him not to mention his age but he had defied her.

His first raid had been at night, hitting a small settlement where the government soldiers had carried off the men. There was no stealth – the boys stumbled through the straggly bush until the firing started. Gabriel's legs buckled under him but he forced himself forward. Amid the screaming of the women and children he closed his eyes and fired into the dark. The air was thick with smoke and there was a constant buzzing in his ears that would stay with him for days.

'You think you're too good for us don't ya? Slut.' The boys were growing bolder.

Gabriel rose slowly to his feet and walked the six rows to the boys. He stopped in the aisle and stood quietly above the group, his hands by his side. He felt the lost familiar unhinging of time, the crackling of nerves just below his skin and the heightened attention to detail – a blink, a sideways glance, a too-short breath. The sweet stillness before movement.

'Are you okay, miss?'

The tall boy looked up at him and drew heavily on his cigarette.

'Here we go then,' he said. 'A fuckin' hero'.

Gabriel looked at the girl and spoke again, 'Are you okay, miss?'

'Course she's okay. Why don't you fuck off and leave us alone ya...'

Gabriel noted the hesitation at the end of the sentence, the way it tilted a delicate balance.

The boy looked at the bunched muscles of Gabriel's forearms and the deep scar that wove its way down his wrist and across the back of his right hand. His hands were enormous.

The carriage paused - the rhythmic foomp foomp of the wheels passing over sleepers, the sudden dimming as the train entered a tunnel, the soft swinging of the overhead straps – all slowed in time by the collective holding of breath.

'Ah, stuff ya,' the boy said, 'we were just havin' some fun. Come on boys.'

He made a show of getting to his feet slowly but Gabriel saw the way he couldn't hold his gaze. As the three boys tried to move past him he held his ground, forcing them to climb over the seats.

Gabriel looked back to the girl. 'Thank you,' she mouthed. He sat down and they rode in silence for while, swaying evenly with the rhythm of the train.

'Where are you from?' she asked.

'Sydenham,' he replied politely.

She laughed but caught herself. 'I'm sorry. I... I mean, what country?'

He smiled, a brief flash of white teeth. 'I know what you meant.'

Brenda Saunders

KAFKA'S ROOM

It is not necessary to leave the house. Remain at your table and listen. Do not even listen, only wait ... be wholly still and alone. The world will present itself to you for unmasking, it can do no other...

Franz Kafka

The room is no longer empty. No one has been here. The last people moved out long ago. There is no sound, but you are aware of a presence in the chair, the space it occupies, feel the weight of a body pressed against the seat, the warmth rising from the velvet cover. You wonder is this the chair he once sat in? You can't see any dust on the wooden frame, in fact it has a polished look, the shine of a favourite chair darkened by many fingers. There is an indentation on the heavy carpet, a sign of his feet planted firmly on the floor. You reach out, feel a coolness under your fingers. He is leaning forward now, elbows and hands hover at the table. A blue light stirs the air, fills the room. The door is closed and there are no windows. No way out. It was the same yesterday and every day before that.

Julie Chevalier

THE MAN WHO WALKS
AFTER WORK

what is so rare as a day in june   a steak?   then   if
ever come perfect   northern hemisphere of course   james
russell lowell   grandpa's favourite poet a tim tam for lines
memorised   *& over it softly a warm ear*   absolute crap:
heaven having warm ears   *hear life murmur or see it glisten*
glisten like the wetlands   dragonflies an indication the water's
clean   no turtles today   never seen a blue-tongue like that
methadonian in the shop this morning   *someone stole my*
'done & don't i know who it was   leftrightleftright   never told
us in pharmacology lectures   heard a poet on the radio walk in
iambic pentameter   the pace of blood   the pace of breathing
a water bottle hanging from that bloke's waistband   pulls a
good pair of strides right out of shape   no way to keep shoes
from squeaking

new rubbish in the lane   a dumped baby's shoe   lights in
windows   two dollar kitsch in the yard   christmas beads   love
hearts   kid's whistle   warning: cedric the dog: do not steal
angels & mermaids & madonnas   toy airplane on a branch

as lila said at surfers' airport   *no piece of yellow plastic with a whistle ever saved a life*   been gone three weeks

young street   *all right, thanks, yourself?*   terraces with heritage indian takeaway menus blowing   left right left right   stimulate enzymes to burn LDL   walk too fast to sustain   if anyone to talk to   dog walkers stop-starting   *hello there! how's little patrick today?*   new collar patrick?   insult naming a dusty mop after a nobel prize winner

styles street   *evening*   *no, no, don't know what she's up to* thank goodness the flat's in my name   body corporate meeting dog turd on my best   she's probably somewhere detoxing garden bins should have been emptied sunday

mostly bills   press three   yes key in pocket   the light, that's better   her ikea magazine   berlin family squashed in two rooms of dinosaur toys   how many zany vases does one family with no garden   lila expected consolation roses each time her period started   forgot dental floss again

she cut a whole room of baby furniture from the catalogue   an hour to choose a night light   no sense buying a striped circus tent for a kid who hasn't been conceived   set up my one-man tent in the second bedroom   *no need to take everything so*

literal   threw her stuff in the tent after she left   she wanted
my baby sure   porn mags   sperm in a bottle   twelve years
younger but   her problem not mine

abc fm & no finer music than johann sebastian   packet carbonara
again   the scissors were here last night   told her *not enough
to give up caffeine if you smoke & drink*   the gulliver cot with
its safety features still in the carton   wanted to call a girl ryder
ryder?   mail her magazine into the tent   could have been an
emma with red curls   should put the cot up on eBay   not yet

Patrick Lenton

PHRASEO- ROGUE EDITOR

Ha ha ha, the name is Phraseo – Rogue Editor. The rumours are true, I was the best editor the Grammar Council possessed, but then like two eggs, I was dropped for no reason. Why, grammar council? We could have eaten those eggs. What do I do now? Ha ha ha, Phraseo spits in the face of The Grammar Council – for not even God can stop him from editing. Phraseo is everywhere, is a shadow; he is editing your street art while you sleep. Phraseo is in your billboards, making advertising less appealing. Phraseo comes into your home and spaces your paragraphs correctly. Phraseo double spaces your personal diary. Phraseo thinks only in Helvetica. He puts the claws back in various grammatical clause.

Ha ha ha – Phraseo, he thinks you are beautiful, like correct use of quotation marks. Ha ha ha, Phraseo has drunk too much in the middle of the day again. Ha ha ha, Phraseo will tell YOU when he's had enough, ha ha ha, Phraseo, he puts the semi back in your colon.

Kevin Gillam

MOTH WORDS

number of sips equals number of tastes. if you were to lie like that, upside down. Chopin saw Bb minor as charcoal. cirrus is a smeared silent language. legs propped against the wall, world. in ICU its your name and the day. smother hides mother holds

other. if you were to sit. raking the coals, making night in the grate. more salve in horizons than creeds. lake gone to seed. ravens prefer to roost on dead branches. thinks spin but a moon librates. eyes and mind in soft focus, all elsewhere. ill's a good

word—deals with it succinctly. we're ants in the blind search for sweetness. if you were to lose sight. congregations of tuarts, all standing. go with wind through leaves and voices. it's a dangerous light near the surface. monks can tell one silence from

another. soles as creeds, forgetting North. not recuperating, always the next. not long after I'm dead you'll be dead. if bark and clouds and blood were text and thoughts came in boats. number of truths equals number of cuts. a peppermint brailles in bark.

and if was as fuller sentence as why. venetians slivering the

mopoke's call. we're all wide-eyed in the sudden light. if you were
to pretend. the undead aren't writing books about it. a hammer
feels the purpose of nail. play, let the hours be plasticine. all

purpled, flywired, Sunday afternooned. can see the black in blue.
the shape of if? while in my shirt box mind pinning moth words

Ron Pretty

TROUT

A westerly gale all night with rain but now the clouds have lifted. The sun is shining and she's leaving. Her pregnant daughter lives up north and she is flying there to be with her. Her only luggage is her heart, much travelled and beaten. The labels on it tell of phone calls and emails from Perth saying it is over, he has left her, he is in the arms of a new lover. He is sorry for the dogs on their chains he left behind, and his motorbikes. She is rising above the city, the ocean shivers and glitters from the storm. The boeing banks and turns, heading towards her daughter's spare bed. He is playing her like a trout, she still hangs on the end of his line. She is flying away from him but he reels her in with threats and promises. He will come home, he will spend all their money, he is so much smarter than she is, he never loved her, he loves her still, Perth is his city and home of his swan, his swain, his heart has caught fire, he has flown away wanting to come back. She welcomes the whine of the engines, she closes her eyes on his text, she has changed the locks on the house, farmed out the dogs to the neighbours. She has promised herself she's starting again, it's over, the Dianella swan can have him. It is finished. After twenty-five years it is finished, she has come of age. She's above the clouds of doubt, she is fleeing to her pregnant daughter. Even if he begged her now . . . She hears the engines change their tune, she begins the descent to the land beyond the border. The boeing touches down, she walks the passage to her patient daughter as her phone begins to ring. She cannot disconnect. He plays her

like a trout.

Nick Couldwell

WESTERLY

His dark figure always made me uneasy. I had to remind myself it was his blurry silhouette out there, legs buried beneath the waves.

I never really fell asleep. Just drifted in and out of consciousness like the white caps out past the breakers, licked by the late-changing westerly. As the night wore on and the wind gailed, sand built up against my sleeping bag, my lips dry and sugared. I hid beneath the dunes and wrapped my body against the wind and sand and darkness.

Sometimes I would wake to find an empty beach in front of me, the damp shoreline forbidding and desolate under the moon's milky light. I scanned the shore and the empty blanket of darkness above the explosions of white, looking for his bobbing glow in the distance.

Our camp was the only blemish on the strip of beach. Tackle boxes and Eskies, blankets and canned soup were sprawled across the sand. My fishing rod lay next to me, restless and unused as it waited to be marched down to the shore. It was always the same; the old man rigged me up a rod even though he knew I wasn't going to use it. Kneeling in the white earth with his tongue pinched between his teeth, he would tie swivels and sinkers by the flare of his head torch. He would pat me on the back and reassure me the wind would swing west and it would be the best wind, the perfect wind for fishing.

Sometimes I snapped up my abandoned rod and rushed at the sound of the waves, his silhouette like a beacon against the backdrop of the wild. The sand screeched between my toes, the sound screaming of long lost adventure and adolescence. The westerly chased me to the shore where I stood knee-deep in the salty wash.

After the first dozen casts, the thrill and excitement ebbed away with the tide. The warmth of father and son, huddled close with our backs to the wind, soon became repetition, almost an annoyance as he waded over to me swearing under my breath at the tangled line and the moon. He let it be though, the swearing. I could tell he wanted to keep me happy, keep me out there as long as he could knowing there wasn't going to be many chances like this.

We stood with our feet buried in the sand, our rods resting against our cold bellies. We threw out random lines about school, about work. We whittled down the minutes with our all-time Manly tries and players, and we laughed with the stars at the thought of Melbourne Storm's nil defeat in last year's Grand Final.

When the all-time greatest moments washed away, fatigue settled in. The mood became solemn and the small talk returned. The water washed over every word, every silence. I turned my head against the howling wind to hear the graveness of my father's voice. I had to shift closer to listen about the first time I stepped into the ring and the hatred my mother had for him letting me get knocked cold. Reckless, she had called it. I'd heard it all before, but this was different. Just by the placidness of his voice, I knew he was trying to tell me something, release some buried burden.

Our lines trailed out to sea, submerged in the roughness, no doubt baitless and untouched. He continued in the same secretive tone and I strained to listen against the sounds of the world, which seemed to be exploding around us. He told me about my dropped ball over the line, seconds before the siren in our under fifteen's grand final. He explained how he had tried to persuade the state selectors who had seen it from the sideline, that it was a one off, a bad fluke. But, that was all they needed to see. The games leading up to the finals where I was the top try scorer didn't matter. Somehow, standing there knee-deep in regret, I felt like this was the time to change it all, to rectify the past mistakes concealed fathoms below the achievements that have since occurred.

The silence between us began to break the roar of the wind. It settled to a stagnant crawl and the lulled ocean shifted tamely around our legs. My dad's old stories and his voice weren't the heavy weight; it was the world, unbalanced and bearing down. The sea was content and crickets hummed deep in the bitou bush behind the dune walls.

I marveled at the stars and the phosphorous in the shallows, drowning below it all, in my own insignificance. Standing there, just us, everything else became oblivious and I knew, I knew this was all that really mattered.

Hilary Hewitt

HAPPY

to stand out in the market (loquats, mulberries, apples, the usual crowd)   hao xianzhang makes special moulds to fit over his embryonic pears   other growers scoff   then watch the sweet-faced baby-shapes sell for 50 yuan each   the third generation of chinese shopper is less price-sensitive and displays high levels of brand loyalty   designer handbags are sought after (armani, burberry, kors)   urban couples have been restricted to one baby   why not pears   18,000 pre-packaged healthy infants   fruit enterprise is encouraged   by the proto-capitalist branch   shoppers decide their happy baby dolls are too cute to eat   the fruit rots   100 million chinese live below the poverty line   the one-child policy is linked to forced abortion and female infanticide   next season hao plans pears shaped like charlie chaplin the choice of celebrity not app(e)arent   a new marketing campaign may be required

TROLLEY JAM

a woman in lime leggings arguing with leopard print chick over a mother's day nightie with appliquéd cats, poor nanna i think. a teenager folds then refolds too many size nothing onesies into too many plastic bags and i want to offer sentences on contraception and recycling, but k-mart demands a choice of queue–cash or card–for my $5 purchase as if kev and tony are in front of me when i want to vote green and pay with challenging words. this week my father turned 96, he told me three times he didn't like my present–too small, wrong colour, round collar– but when i exchanged the jumper for navy blue, XL, v-neck, he praised my good taste as if i was 6, not a 56 year old mother who looks after him too, and then threw in a right wing rant, a reverse birthday present. i know he wants to leave the world a better place for his grandchildren and he can't, it's a mess, but please dad, would you just shut up and, oh god, now the girl in front of me (i thought cash would be quicker) is taking t-shirts in bulk from her trolley, how long will this take. i bought one last week ($4) but when i read the label at home, *made in bangladesh*, i threw it in the bin. so should i tap her on the shoulder and say don't you know they're made in factories that kill workers in bulk. are you listening tony and kev and whoever owns k-mart,

wesfarmers and sears holdings i think. much rejoicing on the
news seventeen days later when a seamstress is pulled from
the rubble wearing hot pink, but what about the 1000 dead. i
want to sit down and cry but my printer is hungry for stories and
i'm guessing this a4 paper isn't recycled or green, probably cost
two orang-utans their home. last night my son told me loudly,
five times, that every politician lies–we all become ranters in
my family–that man is staring at me, am i talking out loud or
are we in a race for the exit. i yelled at my son to leave me
alone with my lentils. mother's day tomorrow and she's dead.
all through k-mart there might be women feeling sad because
of buildings collapsing on workers and dying orang-utans, but
you can choose a diamanté collar for your fluffy schmitzoo and
another american company offers post-rapture pet care for all
the little bitzoos (click life on earth). almost out of words but with
much rejoicing, i reach the front of the queue where someone
has edited the sign on the slotted box next to the register, *return
(h)anger* here and instead of buying printer food i stuff orang-
utan paper into the box and the girl with the trolley looks across,
probably thinking oh oh a maddie, but she winks and turns a
t-shirt inside-out so the label shows those black words and then
she stuffs it into st sear's mouth so i grab a few and help, we just
leave crumpled cotton hanging out, pale as rubble

Philip Hammial

SLAVE

Kept naked in her dungeon, fed scraps, whipped daily. Been here for seven years. With any luck will be here for seven more.

Biographies

Based in Bangalow, **STEVI-LEE ALVER** spends her time surfing, spotting clouds, playing pool, watching waves, studying at Southern Cross University, and nursing at the North Coast Cancer Institute. She is currently on exchange at the University of Massachusetts, Amherst.

KATE ANDREWS-DAY is a writer, and the founder and editor-in-chief of *Sarsaparilla Press*, a publishing company focusing on emerging artists and writers. Kate is working on her first novel, about an isolated community-turned-cult in regional NSW.

CASSANDRA ATHERTON is a writer and critic. She has written a book of poetry, *After Lolita* (Ahadada Press, Tokyo and Toronto, 2010); a novel, *The Man Jar* (Printed Matter Press, New York and Tokyo, 2010) and her prose poems have recently appeared in *Best Australian Poems 2012* and *2013*.

Moroccan born, **KATHLEEN BLEAKLEY** is returning to Wollongong after Canberra years. Her craft is influenced by Joanne Burns through Creative Writing @ University Of Wollongong. Kathleen's publications include *jumping out of cars* with Andrea Gawthorne & 'pling.

JUDE BRIDGE has a penchant for the ridiculous and the evil. She was beyond thrilled to appear in *The Big Issue Fiction Edition* (2013) and is regularly published in *that's life* magazine.

JULIE CHEVALIER writes poetry and short fiction in Sydney. Her third book, *Darger: his girls* (Puncher & Wattmann) won the *Alec Bolton Prize*. It was short-listed for the WA Premier's Poetry Prize, 2013. juliechevalier.net

MOYA COSTELLO, lecturer, Southern Cross University. Books: *Harriet Chandler* (SOP), *The office as a boat* (Brandl & Schlesinger), *Small ecstasies* (UQP), *Kites in Jakarta* (Sea Cruise), Recently in *Stoned Crows & other Australian Icons* (Spineless Wonders, 2013), *Griffith Review*. Co-editor, *Mud map* (Text).

LAUREN AIMEE CURTIS is a writer from Sydney. Her short fiction has appeared in *Going Down Swinging*, *Two Serious Ladies*, *New World Writing*, and the UTS writers' anthology *Hide Your Fires*.

ROMANA DALGLIESH is a year into her PhD at RMIT. Her research focuses on issues of authorial control in narrative nonfiction writing, particularly sudden memoir, where flash nonfiction is used to limit narrative to glimpses of recent private moments.

ALEXIA DERBAS is a twenty-two year old writer from Sydney. She has a Bachelor of Media and Communications, majoring in Writing and Cultural Studies. This will be her first published piece of fiction.

KEVIN GILLAM is a West Australian writer with three books of poetry published. He works as Director of Music at Christ Church Grammar School and as a freelance cellist.

LINDA GODFREY is an editor, judge and publicist for Spineless Wonders and she hosts the South Coast NSW poetry event, *Rocket Readings*. Linda holds a Masters in Professional Writing

(University of Technology, Sydney). She is published in *Cordite* and audio anthologies by River Road Press.

NICK COULDWELL is 24 years old. He was born and lives in Byron Bay with his partner and daughter. He studied professional writing and editing at RMIT and is currently writing a novel.

PHILIP HAMMIAL has had 26 collections of poetry published, two of which were short-listed for the *Kenneth Slessor Prize* and one for the *ACT Poetry Book Prize.* He has represented Australia at eight international poetry festivals, most recently at Granada, Nicaragua in February 2014.

JONATHAN HADWEN is a Brisbane writer whose poetry has been published in *Westerly*, *fourW*, and *foam:e*, as well as other publications in Australia and overseas.

TIM HEFFERNAN lives close to the edge – the piece of land sitting between the escarpment and the continental shelf. He has had more success with e-zines than green bottles and so some of his poetry is online.

HILARY HEWITT lives and works in Sydney's inner west. She was shortlisted in the *2012 Overland Victoria University Overland Short Story Prize for New and Emerging Writers* and the *Margaret River Short Story Competition 2013.*

ELIZABETH HODGSON is a Wiradjuri woman and her book *Skin Painting* won the David Unaipon in 2007. Her poetry is published in several anthologies. American LED artist, Jenny Holzer has selected some of Elizabeth's poems for permanent display in Chifley Square in Sydney.

RICHARD HOLT coordinates *Flashing the Square*, a microfiction video project for public screens. He writes microfiction, poetry and longer form fiction and blogs about microfiction (bigstorysmall.com). He was a cofounder of the zine store, *Sticky*.

ALANA KELSALL lives in Melbourne.In 2010/11 she was shortlisted for the *Newcastle Poetry Competition* and commended in the *Rosemary Dobson Prize*. She is now working on her first solo collection of poetry.

PARICK LENTON writes prose and theatre and blogs at *The Spontaneity Review* and the *Rory Gilmore Reading Challenge*. He is a digital marketer at *Momentum Books*. @patricklenton

MARJORIE LEWIS-JONES is a Sydney-based writer, editor and poet. She works in publishing and media management, has run creative writing and journalism workshops and is a voracious reader and reviewer with eclectic tastes. She blogs about books, reading and writing at a biggerbrighterworld.com.

JOSHUA LOBB's stories have appeared in *The Bridport Anthology*, *Best Australian Stories*, *Text* and *Social Alternatives*. His plays have been performed at The Actor's Centre and Belvoir St Theatre. He is currently completing a massively over-populated novel, *Remission*.

NATASHA LUKA is a creative writing student who has received places in local writing competitions and has short stories in several anthologies including *Azuria* and *Imagine*. natashaluka.wordpress.com

SUSAN MCCREERY is a short story writer, poet and proofreader from Thirroul, NSW. She was awarded an *Australian Society*

of Authors Mentorship in 2013–14 to work on her short story collection.

ALYSON MILLER teaches literary studies at Deakin University, Geelong. Her short stories and poetry have appeared in both national and international publications, along with a book of literary criticism, *Haunted by Words: Scandalous Texts* (2013). Her collection of prose poems, *Dream Animals*, is forthcoming with Dancing Girl Press.

JENNI NIXON is a poet and performer. Her work is published in *café boogie* (interactive press 2004) *agenda!* (picaro press 2009) and included in many anthologies and journals. She is a member of company of writers and roundtable writing groups.

MARK O'FLYNN has published four collections of poetry, plus three novels including *Grassdogs* and *The Forgotten World*. He has also published the comic memoir *False Start*. A collection of short fiction, *White Light*, was published by Spineless Wonders in 2013.

RON PRETTY's eighth book of poetry, *What the Afternoon Knows*, was published in 2013. A revised and updated version of his *Creating Poetry* will be published later this year.

MARK ROBERTS is a Sydney based writer and critic. He is a founding editor of *P76 magazine* and currently edits *Rochford Street Review*. He has two chapbooks due for release before the end of the year.

BRENDA SAUNDERS is a Sydney poet and artist of Aboriginal and British descent. She has published three collections of poetry, her most recent *the sound of red* (Ginninderra Press

2013). She recently returned from a Resident Fellowship at CAMAC Arts Centre in France.

ALI JANE SMITH is a poet and critic. Her work has appeared in *Southerly, Cordite, Famous Reporter* and other journals. She is the author of the chapbook *Gala* (Five Islands Press 2006). She lives in Wollongong.

MARK SMITH lives on Victoria's West Coast. His writing has appeared in *Visible Ink, Offset, Mascara, Margaret River Press* and *Award Winning Australian Writing*, among others. He also finds it a little strange talking about himself In the third person.

ANDREW STUCKGOLD is a writer and photographer living in Erskineville N.S.W. He is currently working toward completing a postgraduate degree in Creative Writing at Sydney University.

The joanne burns Award

Each year Spineless Wonders auspices an award for the best writing in the forms of prose poem and microfiction in honour of foremost Australian experimental poet, joanne burns. The award is open to people residing in Australia and to Australians living overseas. Finalists chosen by each year's judging panel are offered publication in our annual anthology alongside invited writers.

The *2013 joanne burns Award* was judged by Shady Cosgrove who selected Mark Smith's '10.42 to Sydenham' as the winning entry and Hilary Hewitt's 'happy' and Mark Robert's 'cities that are not Dublin' as runners-up. All three pieces, along with those of other finalists appear in *Writing to the Edge*, edited by Linda Godfrey and Ali Jane Smith.

The *2012 joanne burns Award* was judged by Carol Jenkins who selected Mark O'Flynn's 'under the maw of luna park' as the winning entry and commended Richard Holt's 'bush burial', Trina Denner's 'playing outside', Stu Hatton's 'down south' and Paul Mitchell's 'The Old Man and the Pool'. The winner and finalists all appear in *Stoned Crows & other Australian Icons*, edited by Julie Chevalier and Linda Godfrey.

The inaugural *joanne burns Award* was held in 2011 and was judged by joanne burns who selected Charles D'Anastasi's

'Madame Bovary' as the winning entry and commended Erin Gough's 'William Shatner vows to save the Great Basin Pocket Mouse' and Clare McHugh's 'Briefly'. All three pieces, along with those of other finalists appear in *small wonder*, edited by Linda Godfrey and Julie Chevalier.

In *2014, the joanne burns Award* was judged by Angela Meyer and Richard Holt and the winner and runners up will be published in *Flashing the Square*, edited by Linda Godfrey and Bronwyn Mehan.

ABOUT JOANNE BURNS

joanne burns grew up in Sydney's eastern suburbs. She worked as an English teacher in New South Wales, and for a time in London. She has taught creative writing in tertiary institutions, schools and community organisations. Her first collection of poems, *Snatch*, was published in London in 1972. Since then she has published more than a dozen further books of poetry. Her poems have appeared in numerous Australian literary journals, poetry magazines and have been set for study on the Higher School Certificate syllabus. joanne has been particularly concerned with the blurring of the distinctions between poetry and prose in her work, and has written extensively in prose poem/ microfiction forms. She has also written monologues and short futurist fictions and 'farables' (fables/ parables).Her forthcoming collection is *Brush*, (Giramondo Poets, 2014))

Also from

Spineless Wonders

Small Wonder
prose poems & microfiction

edited by Linda Godfrey and Julie Chevalier

Here are short and clever pieces by thirty contemporary Australian writers on the eroticism of mashed potato, parenting as magic realism and a tongue-in-cheek history of the Cyclops bicycle. Includes award-winning writers Michael Farrell, Keri Glastonbury, Judith Beveridge and Peter Boyle. Features prose poems and microfiction selected by competition judge joanne burns.
Illustrated by talented young artist, Paden Hunter.

Stoned Crows
& other Australian Icons
prose poems & microfiction

edited by Linda Godfrey and Julie Chevalier

What do our best wordsmiths have to say about Australian icons? This anthology takes a fresh look at everything from the HIH collapse to crocs, Margaret Olley, bush burials and the ABC. We visit a post-apocalyptic Opera House and spend Saturday night in downtown Byron Bay. Tones range from nostalgic to sceptical, from wry to LOL. Featuring prose poems and microfiction by Mark O'Flynn, Anna Kerdijk Nicholson, Michael Sharkey, Moya Costello and many more.

EARWORMS
short Australian audio

Stories that stay with you

Earworms are those songs with unforgettable hooks that get stuck in your head but Spineless Wonders brings you short Australian earworms—stories by award-winning writers that you definitely won't want to forget.

Stuck in a queue? Don't stress. You can listen to our selection of funny, political and thought-provoking prose poems and microfiction from our anthology, *Small Wonder*.
Got a pile of washing-up or ironing to do? Housework's not a chore when you have an audio story.

Commuting every day? Traffic jams are not a problem when you can listen to the latest in contemporary short fiction from Spineless Wonders.

Prices range from $0.99 to $2.99. Gift vouchers available.

Listen to our audio trailers now at
www.shortaustralianstories.com.au.

Spineless Wonders publications are available in print and digital format from participating bookshops and online. For further information about where to purchase our print, audio and ebooks, go to the Spineless Wonders website:

www.shortaustralianstories.com.au